This
PJ BOOK
belongs to

_____

_____

PJ Library®

JEWISH BEDTIME STORIES and SONGS

For my grandsons,
Jacob, Yoni, Andrew,
and Aaron
— DA

For Finley and Mitch
— JE

Apples & Honey Press
An imprint of Behrman House and Gefen Publishing House
Behrman House, 11 Edison Place, Springfield, New Jersey 07081
Gefen Publishing House Ltd., 6 Hatzvi Street, Jerusalem 94386, Israel
www.applesandhoneypress.com

Text copyright © 2015 by David A. Adler
Illustrations copyright © 2015 by Behrman House, Inc.

ISBN 978-1-68115-500-5

Library of Congress Cataloging-in-Publication Data
Adler, David A.
Hanukkah cookies with sprinkles / by David A. Adler ; illustrated by Jeffrey Ebbeler.
pages cm
Summary: Sara learns about the Jewish tradition of tzedakah
when she shares food with a hungry stranger.
ISBN 978-1-68115-500-5
[1. Charity--Fiction. 2. Jews--United States--Fiction. 3. Judaism--Customs and
practices--Fiction. 4. Hanukkah--Fiction.] I. Ebbeler, Jeffrey, illustrator. II. Title.
PZ7.A2615Han 2015
[E]--dc23
2014026408

Design by David Neuhaus/NeuStudio
Edited by Dena Neusner
Printed in China

1 3 5 7 9 8 6 4 2
111515.9K1/B0749/A6

Hanukkah Cookies
with
Sprinkles

By David A. Adler

Illustrated by
Jeffrey Ebbeler

APPLES & HONEY PRESS

Springfield, NJ • Jerusalem

Every morning I watch by the window as Mom goes to work.

She leaves our building and walks past Sol's Market to the bus stop. Before she gets on the bus, she turns, looks up, and waves to me.

I wave back. I stay there and see other people hurrying to work. I stay there until Grandma says, "Sara, it's time to get ready for school."

While I look out the window, I see Sol open his store. He loads the tables in front. He finds a few bad fruits and vegetables and puts them in a box. He can't sell them, so he puts them on the side of the store.

One day I see an old man look in the box. He takes out an apple and puts it on his shoulder. The apple rolls down his arm and into his hand. Then he takes a bite.

"Why did he eat that apple?" I ask Grandma. "It has lots of bad spots."

"It has lots of good spots, too," Grandma says. "That man is probably poor and looking for something to eat."

I think about him eating around the bad spots on the apple. He must be very hungry.

I think about him when I eat breakfast and when I walk with Grandma to school.

At school we play and learn about letters, numbers, and holidays.

At snack, my teacher gives me a cookie and milk. I look at my cookie and think about the man. I wrap my cookie in a napkin and put it in my pocket.

At supper I tell Mom about the man. I show
her the cookie.

"Could you leave it for him?" I ask.

The next morning Mom puts the cookie in a bag.
She leaves it by the side of Sol's store.

Later I see the man open the bag. He takes out the cookie, spins it on the tip of his finger, and eats it.

At school I tell my friends about him, and we wrap lots of cookies. My teacher says she's proud of us. She says what we're doing is called tzedakah. We're giving to someone who has less than we have.

My teacher gives tzedakah, too. She gives me a container of juice for the man.

That night I help Mom make him a sandwich.

The next morning he finds the cookies, juice, and sandwich. He looks around. I think he wants to know who has left him such good things. This is the first time I see his face, and I think I've seen him before. I just don't know where.

On Friday night Mom and Grandma light Shabbat candles. Then we go to synagogue. After the service there's an *oneg Shabbat*. It's like a Shabbat party. And guess what? I see him.

"Mom, Grandma," I whisper.

"What, Sara?" they ask.

"I know that man. That's him."

The man eats some challah. He drinks some grape juice. We all do.

After that, every day, when the man comes by Sol's, there is something for him to eat.

Then one day my teacher says Hanukkah is coming.

I love Hanukkah. It's a happy holiday.

"On Hanukkah," my teacher says, "we light candles for eight nights. We remember the fight for freedom many years ago. We remember the fight so Jews could light Shabbat candles and study the Torah. We also remember how a small bit of oil burned and burned."

She gives us each some tiles, bottle caps, paint, and glue.

"We're making menorahs," she says. "You can use them at home to light Hanukkah candles."

Just before the first night of Hanukkah,
I bring my menorah home.

"It's beautiful," Grandma says.

I know it is.

Grandma sets it by the window.

"We'll light the candles and play dreidel
when Mom comes home," Grandma says.

"Now, let's make latkes and Hanukkah cookies."
Latkes are potato pancakes.

"Let's make extra," I say.

We make a lot of latkes.

We bake lots of cookies in the shapes of menorahs and dreidels.

I cover them with sprinkles!

Mom comes home, and I show her
my new menorah.

"It's beautiful," Mom says. "But what
about the one you made last year?"

She takes it from the cabinet.

It's also beautiful.

"Take it with you when you go to work,"
I say. "Put it by the trash near the fruit store."

"Don't throw it out," Grandma says.

"I'm not," I tell her. "I'm giving tzedakah. I'm giving it to someone who has less than we have."

The next morning, the man takes the menorah out of the bag and looks at it. There are also latkes, cookies with sprinkles, and Hanukkah candles. I see that the man's cheeks are a little wet. I hope those are happy tears.

On Friday, Mom and Grandma prepare a special Shabbat and Hanukkah dinner with lots of good things to eat. At synagogue that night, I want to invite the man to our house for dinner.

"But, Sara," Mom says, "we don't know him. He's a stranger."

"Please," I say.

Mom and I speak to the rabbi. He knows the man.

"His name is Morris Berger," the rabbi tells us. "I've known him for a long time. He's here every Friday afternoon to set up the chairs. After Shabbat he puts away all the books."

The rabbi introduces Mom and me to Mr. Berger.

Mom asks him, "Would you like to join us for a homemade Shabbat and Hanukkah dinner?"

"Please," I say.

Mr. Berger smiles.

He comes home with us.

He talks a lot during dinner. He lives nearby, in a small apartment. He once worked in a circus. He shows me some tricks the clowns had taught him. He juggles some small pieces of challah. Then one by one he catches each piece of challah in his mouth and eats it.

I wish I could juggle.

Mom brings out dessert, a plateful of Hanukkah cookies all covered with sprinkles. Now Mr. Berger knows who has been leaving cookies, sandwiches, and milk for him. He knows who left him the menorah and candles.

At first Mr. Berger looks down. I think he's a little embarrassed. Then he looks at me and says in a real quiet voice, "Thank you."

"Mr. Berger," I say, "I hope you'll visit again."

"I'd like that," he says, "and please call me Morris."

Mom tells him to have another cookie.

"I will," he says. "But first I'll show you some more magic."

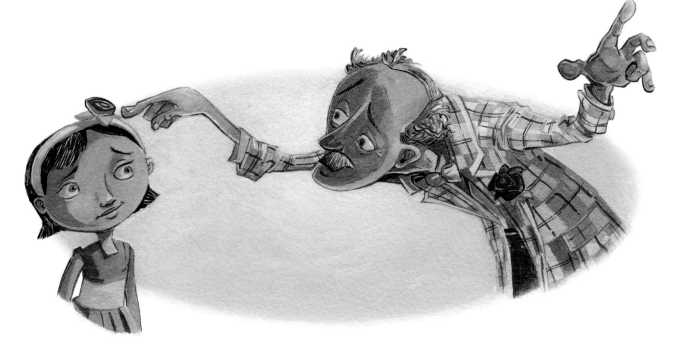

Morris reaches behind my ear and takes out a Hanukkah cookie with sprinkles.

"Now watch this. I'll make it disappear."

He takes one big bite and the cookie is gone.

"That's okay," I say. "We have lots more.
We have lots to share."

"I also have things to share," Morris says. "I can teach you some easy magic tricks. I can tell you funny circus stories."

"Can you teach me to juggle?"

Morris laughs.

"I can try," he says. "But juggling takes lots of practice."

"Sara will need lots of juggling lessons," Mom says.

Morris smiles. He knows that lots of lessons mean lots more Shabbat dinners with us.